The Noisy Farm

Lots of animal noises to enjoy!

by Marni McGee

illustrated by Leonie Shearing

BLOOMSBURY
CHILDREN'S
BOOKS

Farming Times

Tractor driver 'Out of Control' Ploughs wrong field

Cows storm through Village

Food + Farming

For my lovely, loving daughter Elizabeth T. McGee
and in memory of my grandfather William Earl Broach – MM

To dearest Poppa and the animals he adored – LS

BLOOMSBURY
CHILDREN'S
BOOKS

First published in Great Britain in 2004 by Bloomsbury Publishing Plc
38 Soho Square, London, W1D 3HB

Text copyright © Marni McGee 2004
Illustrations copyright © Leonie Shearing 2004
The moral rights of the author and illustrator have been asserted

A CIP catalogue record of this book is available from the British Library
ISBN 0 7475 6424 8

Designed by Sarah Hodder
Colour Separation by Bright Arts Graphics, Singapore

Printed in Hong Kong by South China Printing Co

1 3 5 7 9 10 8 6 4 2

In a pocket of earth between two hills
a quiet farmer lives on his land,
far from the bustle of town.
And when, in the morning, the sun first appears,
the rooster begins to crow.
Cock-a-doo, cock-a-doo! Cock-a-doodle-doo!

Hearing the rooster's bugle call,
the quiet farmer opens his eyes.

He stretches and gets out of bed.

Squeak!

Squeak go the bedsprings.
Creak goes the floor.

Creak!

The yellow cat begins to purr.
Purr-purr. The quiet farmer kneels.
He picks her up and holds her close.

The farmer knows there's work to do.
He dresses and goes outside.
And as he walks down to the barn,
a pail bumps against his knee.
Pong, pong, poink! Pong, pong, poink!

Pong Poink!

'*Moo-moo!*' Old Bessie says.
The quiet farmer sits.

Spling-splosh goes the milk
up to the top of the pail.
The farmer fills a little bowl to give to the yellow cat.
Lip-lap, lip-lap, lip-lap.
The farmer rubs Old Bessie's neck.

Next the chickens must be fed.
Puck-puck, puckety-puck!
The quiet farmer gathers eggs
and puts them in his basket.

Snee Snort.

The horses in the stable snort.
Snee-snort, snee-snort!

They stamp their hooves to ask for grain.
Thump-thump! Thumpety-thump!
The quiet farmer feeds them all.

Now that all his friends have been fed,
the quiet farmer feeds himself.
The kitchen sings a breakfast song.

Gurgle goes the coffee pot.
The frying pan says, '*Sizzle!*'
The porridge on top of the hob says,
'*Bubble-de-blip, bubble-de-blop!*'

With breakfast done, it's back to work.
The quiet farmer goes to the field
and sets the tractor roaring.
Vroom-vroom-vroom!

Vroom-Vroom

The quiet farmer ploughs,
and then he scatters the seed.
Soo-swish, soo-swish, soo-swish!
All through the day, the farmer works.
He hoes. *Scritch-scratch!*
He mows. *Click-clack!*

Oink! Oink!

At dusk the farmer feeds his pigs.
Oink-oink! Squeal-squoink!
They *squish* and *squash* in barnyard mud.

The quiet farmer mops his brow
and decides his work is done.
But then he sees the fence needs mending.
He takes his tools
and nails the boards in place.
Whop-whop-bang! Whop-whop-bang!

When all his chores are finally done,
the quiet farmer folds his hands
and strolls to the farmhouse door.
He stops for a moment to listen and look.

The farm is in shadow, yet lit by stars.
The wind is whistling 'round the barn.
A nightingale is singing.

The quiet farmer smiles.
At last he speaks with words.
'Goodnight,' he says.

my cat

'Goodnight to my rooster,

Good

and my cow.

Goodnight to the stars,

the wind

n j g h t!

and the plough.

Goodnight, goodnight –
it's time to sleep now!'

The quiet farmer goes upstairs.

He puts on his nightshirt
and gets ready for bed.

Squeak!

Creak goes the floor.
Squeak go the bedsprings.

Creak!

The farmer crawls under the covers
and pulls them up to his chin.
The moon shines through the window,
casting a silver glow.

whoo whoo whoo!

Outside an owl is calling, '*Whoo-whoo-whooo!*'
But the farmer does not answer.

His eyes are closed. His breath is deep.
The quiet farmer is fast asleep.